Lisa of Florence

C. T. HAYES

Lisa of Florence

Copyright © 2025 by C. T. Hayes

Published by HIPG, Ltd., Atlanta, GA 30097.

Editorial: Nanette Littlestone
Cover and Interior Design: Peter Hildebrandt

ISBN (print book): 979-8-9915890-3-1
ISBN (e-book): 979-8-9915890-5-5
ISBN (audiobook): 979-8-9915890-6-2

Dedication

In appreciation of my family, for their love and support.

Prologue

It has been suggested that the Mona Lisa painting was commissioned by my husband and painted by Master Leonardo da Vinci. But this is not so, but for the love my husband bears me. He created this fiction to protect my honor, his name, and that of my children. But the true story of how this painting came to be is written in these pages. It is a story of my awakening to who I am, my desire and passion for a life of my own. And of my love for Francesco.

My name is Lisa del Giocondo of Florence. I am old now, but as a young girl my heart yearned for beauty and its expression in paintings and art. These things were forbidden to girls like me, for girls of my age were expected to marry and to have children and to pour all their passion and desire into them. I found that notion to be suffocating.

My father knew how I regarded what lay before me—a quiet life of matrimony and childbearing, with only the joys associated to my place in the shadow of my husband.

But then came Leonardo da Vinci.

Chapter 1

SPRING 1503, FLORENCE

A breeze blew in my window from the Arno River. The fragrance of spring calla lilies and daffodils filled the air together with the pungent smell of the fisheries that lined the riverbanks. On most days I would be indoors studying with my tutor but today was beautiful and the first of the spring days in Florence. After insistent appeal on my part, Father had reluctantly given in, releasing me early from the routine of my studies and granting his permission for me to enjoy the day outside in the city square of the Mercato Vecchio.

Church bells rang out over the city as Beatrice and I made our way along the Via Larga towards the Mercato Vecchio.

Beatrice had been my friend for as long as I could remember. Both of our fathers were bankers in the city of Florence. She was fourteen years old, only one year younger than I, and we spent each day in study with our tutors and the rest of the time in prayer and devotional instruction in the chapel at Santa Trinita. Or that's where Father thought I was. But in truth, we would go to the Mercato Vecchio, a place alive with throngs of people that came from miles around to buy the wool and silk for which the city was famous. Cloth merchants lined the streets with their trestle tables of colorful bolts of purple, crimson, and cerulean. Amidst the din of buyers and sellers there were stalls of vegetables and fruits from the countryside. Freshly caught fish from the Arno River. Rounds of cheese and caskets of imported wine from Chianti. And my favorite, the cook shops, with freshly baked breads and simmering meats that filled the air. But the best thing about it was the news about the people of the city. It seemed to flow through the place like a river.

Bea and I were in a market stall looking through hair combs and leather gloves when I looked up and noticed he was staring at me. He stood there among the purveyors and shop owners as a stream of people flowed around him.

He wasn't dark and handsome in a classic way but possessed a charm that was controlled, seductive, and alluring. A smile played across his face like he had some private amusement. I smiled back and turned away from his gaze. I felt my cheeks warm and knew I was blushing.

When I gathered up the courage to look again he had turned away in profile, and I could see the contour of his face framed by a long beard, thoughtful eyes, and hair that fell to his shoulders. He just stood in the Mercato Vecchio with his hands behind his back, observing everything. He had a demeanor that made him look like he was above it all, yet there was a grace about him.

I knew who he was because Father had spoken of him often. In fact, everyone knew who he was. It was the talk of the city that he had returned from Milan where he had served in the brilliant court of Duke Ludovico Sforza. He was Signore Leonardo da Vinci. Master da Vinci, as he was called. According to Father, he had first been hired to instruct the duke's son, Maximilian, in the art of painting and sculpture. Master da Vinci had been an unknown then. Father said da Vinci then went on to paint many great works for the duke and his royal family when his court was the most magnificent in all Italy. But that was many years ago, for Ludovico's fall from grace is well known by all, and many of the artisans the duke supported left Milan, Master da Vinci among them. And it was for this reason he had returned to Florence.

"They say he painted Duke Ludovico's lovers," Beatrice whispered.

"No one we know has ever seen any of the paintings," I said. "Really, you are such a gossip."

"Some say he is the painter of mistresses," she continued. "If Duke Ludovico's son, Maximilian, wanted him to paint your portrait, would you not let him capture your likeness so Maximilian could dream of you?" As she spoke, she came behind me and enfolded her arms around me as if it were young Maximilian holding me close, her chin resting atop my head, for she was a head taller than me. I pushed her away.

"You're a hopeless romantic, Bea." But I had to admit from then on I thought of the mysterious Master da Vinci. I imagined he had been looking at me because he had seen some beauty in me.

Father says I am beautiful like my mother, but I don't remember her well. I was told she had been a beauty. Father said she had a mane of chestnut hair and olive skin like mine, but she was tall and thin, whereas I am short and of average build. Others have said my nose is too long for my face or my chin too small. So I am unsure if my looks are comely and pleasing to others. Master da Vinci had painted some of the most beautiful women in the land. Surely he knew true beauty when he saw it. Perhaps he saw something in me no one else had seen. That special thing that made men long for a woman. Secretly. I wondered what it was like to be painted as the object of someone's affection.

"Have you not ever wondered what it would be like to be a courtesan?" Bea whispered, clutching my arm.

"Certainly not," I said. "Such things are against God's church."

"I know, but just to think on such things is not a sin."

"Some say it is."

"Don't be a prude, Lisa. Your face is turning red."

I wrenched my arm away from her. "Really, Bea, I am bored with this conversation." I quickened my pace, but Bea matched me easily with long-legged strides that strained against the folds of her gown.

"Just the other day you said you wished someone yearned for you so much that their heart would grow weak at the thought of being without you."

"I did not," I snapped, not meaning to but Bea could be annoying.

But I had said that and more. I wanted to be desired and yearned for. I wanted to be loved passionately. Was that not every girl's dream? But I knew I should take more care with what I told Bea or everyone in the neighborhood would know.

She sighed. "One of us has to be a romantic," she said. "You are going to die an old maid if you don't stop turning away suitors."

Bea didn't understand, for there was always a procession of admirers fawning after her. To look at us together was a picture of opposites.

Bea was beautiful with a heart-shaped face and pale complexion. She was tall and graceful, like her mother. Her hair was flaxen gold with ringlets that fell to her shoulders.

When I walked in the market with Bea, men noticed her beauty, and often I felt like they looked through me to admire her. Because we were the daughters of bankers, we could only marry sons of bankers, for in the city of Florence bankers were held in high esteem. "Not quite royalty but close," Father liked to say.

Our family was of the noble Gherardini family from Tuscany with descendants stretching as far back as the ruling patricians of Rome. Father had inherited rich farmlands of wheat and olive groves. But since Florence was now a republic, Father had to set aside his hereditary claims in Florence to join the Banking Guild. Guilds could not be joined or controlled by the nobility in order to allow everyone to be of equal standing.

"What are my choices, Beatrice? They are all such juveniles," I said derisively, sitting down on a bench in the piazza square.

"That's the problem. Most of us have no choice. Our fathers choose for us." She sat down beside me. "But your father allows you to choose from the suitors."

"After Mother died Father promised me that I could choose as long as he approved of my choice."

"Yes, I know," Bea said. "I have heard this before, but now it is an excuse to hide."

"Father has given permission to a few suitors but none of them have persisted. They got bored or something. Truth is, I don't really know." They were all more interested in pleasing Father than me, and whenever I did share my opinion or anything I was interested in, they all seemed to grow quiet.

"I'll tell you what happened. You started talking about your garden. Young men can only stand so much talk about chrysanthemums or whatever you call them."

"My grandmother imported our chrysanthemums from China," I said, "and any man who can't appreciate them would simply be unsuitable." Bea wasn't wrong, though. For all my love of my gardens and flowers, none of it had gotten me closer to what I truly wanted. "Father has grown impatient with me. He says soon I will be too old for a good match and then older men who need heirs will be my only choice."

Bea frowned at the comment. "Oh, Lisa, I could not bear to think of you as a breeding cow for some old man with cold hands."

"Must you play about everything, Bea? This is serious." I turned to walk away from her.

She caught my hand and spun me around. "I'm sorry, Lisa, but you know me. I'm a fool." I smiled at her, for she always knew what to say to lighten my mood. "Go on, tell me what your father said."

"Father says I need to spend more time in prayer to ask God to send me a husband."

"Pray with me then," she said, putting her hands together. "Oh Lord, bring me a handsome man with strong arms and beautiful hair."

"Beatrice! You should not jest about such things. Are you not afraid of God?"

"God has not heard your prayers for a husband. What makes you believe he has heard mine?"

"Truly, Bea, you go too far. Since you mock God without care will you also test Him? I fear for your immortal soul."

"Alright, alright, I'm sorry." She raised her hands in surrender, a smirk upon her long face.

"You had better hope God has not heard your prayers."

I had never prayed for a husband. What about love and passion? Didn't those lead to marriage? Shouldn't a man adore me and long for me? I thought of Mother dying so young, never having really lived. The idea of a husband that didn't truly love me was suffocating. But Father would think me childish if I told him of my feelings. "Accepting obligation is part of growing up," he would say.

Chapter 2

I came down from my rooms and there he was, reclined in a chair in our sala. Master da Vinci's hair and beard were long and grey but immaculately combed. He wore a simple linen tunic and a Burgundian robe of fine material. He sat amid the tapestries and heraldry of our family in the formal room we used to receive only the most important guests and to convey the nobility of our house and standing in the community.

He had come on the invitation of Father to discuss his commission to paint a mural of the Battle of Anghiari in the great Town Hall of the city. Father thought da Vinci gifted but unsuitable because of his reputation for starting great works and leaving them unfinished. The leaders offered the commission to da Vinci with the hope that his fame would help them raise the additional money needed. For this he had agreed to visit the banking families of Florence to share the vision of his work. And that was why he sat in our sala.

Father appeared to greet our guest, and I noticed Father and Master da Vinci were of the same height, both tall, but where da Vinci was square of shoulder and strong, Father was slight and lean with a receding crop of brown and gray hair, his face deeply furrowed, from the years of managing family business. But also, I thought, from the loss of Mother.

"This is my daughter, Lisa," Father said, pointing at me. Da Vinci rose as I was introduced and bowed to me and Father. "Say hello to Master da Vinci, Lisa."

The moment his eyes rested upon me I froze. I could feel my face getting warm again and my mouth opened and closed like I was a fish on a fisherman's hook. I was in awe of him, this great man of the new learning of art in painting, sculptures, and literature that was flourishing everywhere in Italy.

"Speak, child," Father chided.

"Your lord Father has told me of your garden," said Master da Vinci. "I would like to see it, perhaps after dinner."

Finally, I found my voice. "It would be my pleasure, signore," I heard myself say, as though the words came from someone else.

"So, then, it is settled," Father said.

He and da Vinci continued talking about some other matter, and I took my leave to oversee the preparation of dinner. As I left the room, I turned to glance back at da Vinci and found he was already looking at me, and that smile I had seen earlier in the Mercato Vecchio was on his bearded face again.

The servants set out a dark red tablecloth and bright silver dinnerware. The meal was codfish broiled in butter. The servings arrived at the table on warmed plates of bone and silver. Father had selected a Frascati from our wine cellars, clear and white.

"Absolutely delicious!" declared da Vinci as he sampled a piece of the buttery white fish.

"Thank you for the compliment, signore," I said.

"I am sure Master da Vinci has dined far better at Duke Ludovico's table," Father said, looking from me to our guest.

"I was not often invited to dine with the duke," he said, "however his son brought me some of the food served at the table often enough, and it was of the highest quality, to be sure. But I was a servant, there to provide my services to the family as long as they would have me." He spoke levelly with no emotion, as though he stated an obvious fact.

"The duke is a man of the people," said Father. "Admired by many as one who does not place his position above his responsibility for the needs of his city. Even here in Florence we respected him."

"Yes, he was certainly a man *for* the people," da Vinci replied, "but he was not a man *of* them and did not pretend to be. He valued my skill and occasionally my wit and conversation, but he was clear on my function and did not wish to distract me from it."

"So then you only taught Maximilian," I interrupted. "I mean, did you not paint other subjects for the duke?"

"Lisa," Father interjected, "it is not our place to inquire about matters of the duke's family, especially where it concerns his instructions to our guest. You must forgive my daughter's impertinence," he said, shaking his head at me. "As you see, I have indulged her far too often."

Da Vinci looked again at me. "It is quite alright. Based on your description of her garden, she has a creative gift, and curiosity is often part of that gift."

Father beamed with pride at the compliment and conversation continued about the country hills of Tuscany where Master da Vinci was born and of Florence and how the city had changed since da Vinci had visited last.

After dinner, over coffee, black and thick with cream and sweetened with honey, Father turned the conversation back to my garden again. I didn't expect Master da Vinci to be so knowledgeable about roses, and I had to say I was impressed with his study of plants. Father was pleased with da Vinci's stories and anecdotes. He often invited men of learning and study to show he valued such things, but in truth, Father didn't really understand them, he just wanted to appear to be a man of the world.

Carlo, one of Father's trusted men that managed our farmlands, walked in and patiently stood behind him until he was acknowledged. Father waved him forward and Carlo leaned in and whispered in his ear. After a few moments Father sat up in his seat.

"I apologize for the interruption but there is an urgent matter needing my attention. Excuse me, Master da Vinci, I will be but a moment," said Father standing. "Honor our guest with a tour of your garden," he said, looking at me.

I turned and looked at Master da Vinci and then back at Father, who gave me one of his stern looks.

"Yes, Father," I said, standing up from the table.

"Walk this way, signore." My voice quivered. He pushed away from the table, rose, and followed me without a word through the winding path that led to an open cove filled with an array of colors and the soft gurgle of a water fountain.

"These flowers were planted by our ancestors and were most beloved by my grandmother," I said, facing away from him. I heard him come and stand behind me. "She loved them all," I continued, "and would spend hours working here to cultivate them."

"It was you in the market today," he said softly so none of the servants could hear.

"There is a unique blend of flowers here," I said, ignoring his comment. "Lilies, bougainvillea, citrus fruits, gardenias, lavender, jasmine."

Signore da Vinci stepped in beside me and drew a deep breath of the fragrance that filled the cove.

The low trickle of the sounds of water played on the breeze.

"It is wonderful . . . enchanting even," he said, turning to look at me. "So what is it you want to ask? Some point of intrigue about the people I painted for the duke, I suppose?"

My face flushed and I looked away from him. I must have turned a full shade redder.

I gathered up my courage. "Is it true that you painted Duke Sforza's mistress?"

He sighed. "I am old and have given up the idea that young women see a handsome man when they look at me and so I assumed you kept staring at me during dinner because you wanted to know some bit of gossip or intrigue about Duke Sforza," he said calmly. "Only rumors," he said, waving his hand dismissively. "If they were true, would not people such as the duke pay me for both my skill and my silence?

"These unfortunate rumors were started by my rivals, who did not approve of my choice to leave Florence to serve the duke of Milan. I assure you there's little truth in them, as I painted many things for the duke's family and for the monastery of Santa Maria. And yes, a few portraits."

He said these last words as an admission, I observed, and perhaps, because he spoke to me, a young woman, he found no need to protect his honor or reputation.

"So then it could be true," I said, looking directly into his eyes for the first time.

"Your garden is a work of beauty," he said, avoiding provocation. "What is it about a painting that interests you?"

"Unlike my garden, paintings capture beauty and preserve it."

"I have found true beauty to be not just a moment in time," he said, "but the many transitions of a subject." I began to speak, but he raised his hand, motioning for me to give him a moment to explain. "You see, even the beauty of your garden changes. If you were to see it in the morning sunlight it would be different from its beauty in the failing light of the evening dusk. Each of these are a different aspect of its beauty."

I thought for a moment weighing his words. "So then the beauty captured in a painting is only one of many visions of its beauty."

We spoke for a long time and I found myself coming alive as I listened to him, my mind swirling with possibilities I had never thought about. Finally, I said, "Would you paint me, Signore da Vinci?"

He remained silent for a while, as though he had not heard my question. He only looked at me with that smile I had seen before. Then he said, "Of course."

Father returned and took over the conversation, but I didn't remember anything else that was said. I was bursting within at the idea of Signore da Vinci painting me.

Chapter 3

That summer chatter swirled about the Mercato Vecchio over the portrait of Cecilia Gallerani painted by Master da Vinci. She was known to many as the mistress of Duke Ludovico, and it was said the young girl of sixteen years old had tamed the duke. I had not seen Signore da Vinci since he had visited our home, and I began to think I had made it all up in my head. Maybe he had not really promised to paint me at all. Maybe he had just been indulging a young girl's fantasies.

Weeks passed by and Beatrice and I continued to steal away to the Mercato Vecchio after our morning studies. One day, while waiting for Bea to return from the cook shop, I sat looking into the fountain pool enjoying the cool spray of water upon my face, when I saw his reflection behind me. My heart leaped with excitement, but not wanting to seem anxious, I tried to conceal it.

"How is your lord father, Lisa?" he said in his distinct manner.

"He is well, signore, but then you may ask him yourself. He is meeting me here." I didn't know why I told him that, but I didn't want him to think I had been looking for him.

"I have seen you here at the market many times, but never with your father," he said.

I looked away as if that would hide my deception. "He will be along in a few moments," I said. "You will see."

Da Vinci said nothing. His gaze flicked past me and over the crowds of people in the market and then he returned his focus on me. He simply leaned over and handed me a piece of parchment. It was the old material used for writing. Father had been using paper now for many years. I stared down at my hand and began to unfold the document, but he gestured for me to put it away.

"Give my regards to your lord father," he said. He turned and walked away. He was gone as fast as he had appeared. I put the parchment in my purse, but I kept running my finger along the coarse edges of the document all the way home.

That night I couldn't sleep. The moon shined through the window of my room, and I could see dark clouds drift slowly across its bright face. I had not yet opened the parchment. Maybe I wanted to savor its essence or on some level I didn't want to know the next step.

I opened the wooden chest that I kept under my bed and fumbled through its contents in the dim light of my room until my hand felt cloth. I had wrapped the parchment in a cloth of thick velvet. I sat by the window in the moonlight and undid the twine that bound it. The parchment was old, sheepskin perhaps. It had been used and scraped many times, for it was soft and supple to the touch. I held it for a while. I fingered the grainy lines of its letters, and after a time I read its promises. My wandering thoughts lingered on what it would be like. What people might say if they saw the painting of me. What Mother would think if she had lived to see it, and of Father's disappointment.

On the day Master da Vinci was to paint me, our housemaid Nelda, who dutifully reported to Father everything she heard and saw, came to me to inspect what I was wearing. Seldom did I get dressed without her fat fingers tightening my bodice or smoothing my dress. But today she was making a special fuss of what I was wearing. I was annoyed by her presence today because I wanted to dress in clothes that were elegant and refined but not formal. Yet Master da Vinci's letter gave no instructions on what I was to wear.

"Those are not the clothes I laid out for you, signorina," she said impatiently without prompting. I was wearing my favorite green dress and pleated bodice with a burgundy cioppa overgown.

"Yes . . . yes, I saw them, but I don't care to wear those colors today," I said, "and besides, I am already dressed." Our eyes met and she could see defiance on my face, for I could see her wizened old face fall. But she knew her place and said nothing to challenge me.

"Your father won't like it," she said under her breath and turned and left without another word.

I came downstairs ready for my adventure. I found a young man sitting at the dining room table eating. Although he was dressed for hunting, not like a banker, his fine clothes suggested he was from one of the wealthy merchant families. I reasoned he might be here to accompany Father to one of our properties in the country, for he wore rich wool trousers and fine calf length boots and an oiled cape thrown over his shoulders for walking in wet weather.

He stood as I entered. He had a chubby face framed by long blond hair and very light grey eyes, a coloring that was unusual and only seen in Naples to the south.

"Franco," he said with a bow, struggling to speak with his mouth full of brown bread and cheese from our kitchen. I looked at him, not realizing he was speaking to me.

"Franco," he repeated, removing his cap. "Your father said you were beautiful, but I had no idea."

"Thank you," I said despite the unpleasant noise of chewing his bread and cheese. He seemed nice, pleasant even. "Are you here to see Father?"

"Yes, Signorina, I mean sort of," he stammered.

"I will let Father know you are here. Good day, Signore," I said and went out into the garden to pick some flowers for Master da Vinci. The gardenias were in bloom, and he had been taken by their fragrance and beauty.

I had thought nothing of the meeting, but when I came in from the garden, the young man was there talking with Father, chuckling and nodding his head so his long blond hair danced. Father saw me and called me over.

"I would like you to meet Franco. His father serves the Medici family in Florence." Franco inclined his head in acknowledgment of his introduction, a bashful grin wide across his face. "Franco," Father looked to him, "may I present my daughter, Lisa," he said formally. I received his hand in greeting.

"I told your lord father we met earlier." He pulled out a chair for me to sit.

"I have another engagement, Father." I turned to leave.

"You will stay and entertain our guest," he said, giving one of his insistent looks that meant no amount of reasoning would avail. So I sat, resigned to the certainty he would now not allow me to leave for the rest of the day, or until our guest did. One of our servants came and served coffee. I watched Franco sip the hot liquid in a loud slurping noise as he spoke to Father, and for a brief moment I found him quite aggravating. He turned to speak to me with a smile across his chubby face and I was sure then that I was truly annoyed by him.

I lifted my cup of coffee and drank half in a trance while our guest chattered on. Tomorrow, I thought. Tomorrow I would look for Master da Vinci and tell him why I could not come. He would understand. He would give me another chance. Even as I rolled the words over in my head

I did not believe them. Creative men such as da Vinci were creatures of the moment and once their interest wandered elsewhere, they seldom returned.

"Lisa, Franco asked you a question," Father said.

"I am sorry, signore. I am a bit tired. Please continue."

But no matter where the conversation went that day my mind wandered elsewhere. And all through dinner my thoughts were preoccupied with what Master da Vinci would think of my absence. Finally, Franco stood up, announcing he would take his leave. He was visibly disappointed in my lack of interest in him, for the warm smiles he had offered earlier in the day had slowly turned cold. But I could not hide my discouragement of missing my moment with Master da Vinci. It seemed I could not help myself. My behavior was selfish and immature, like a child who had not gotten their way. I soured at all his conversation, responded feebly to his questions, and barely cracked a smile at his humor. Poor Franco. He had been a gentleman, and I had been a brat.

Later in my room I felt very tired. Weary even of all the emotions and frustration of the day. The idea of being painted by Master da Vinci now seemed like a stupid gesture. An adolescent dream of a hopelessly romantic little girl. I was a woman now. No responsible adult would consider such an act. I could not go, of course.

Chapter 4

The next day I awoke tired and unrested. I didn't sleep well, tossing and turning for much of the night. I dressed mechanically and went to the kitchen for a quick breakfast of fruit and cheese. I said my farewells and went off to the monastery for my devotional lessons. When I arrived, Beatrice was waiting for me. I sat in my regular seat amid the sculptures, paintings, and pastel walls of the chapel. I didn't want to speak to her, not wanting to share my disappointment. But she was there, full of life, laughing and blathering on as she always did. I smiled at the flutter of words that poured out of my friend.

"You look tired," she said, sitting in a wooden seat across from me. The morning sunlight played across her slender face so I could see the freckles on her high cheekbones. "Whatever did you do yesterday?"

I paused for a moment as two of the monastery nuns passed by with stern looks on their wrinkled old faces because of all the chatter coming from us. I waited until they passed and lowered my voice to a whisper so only Bea could hear.

"Father entertained a guest," I said, "or perhaps I should say I entertained his guest."

"Long day?" she said.

"Yes, a day that began with a suitor calling upon me."

Bea's face brightened with excitement, for she was always ready to digest tasty bits of gossip. "Did you say suitor?"

"Yes. Father invited him so I had to see to his amusement. Coffee and dinner, and listening to Father tell his stories, enough to make any day last forever."

"What was he like?" Beatrice said suddenly alert and interested, leaning forward to soak up my words.

"He was nice enough, I guess. I don't know."

Annoyance flashed across Bea's face. "You never know. Really, Lisa, stop being so picky," she said irritably.

Perhaps Bea was right. I had been rather difficult to please of late, but after so much disappointment, who could blame me if my expectations were not very high.

"He laughed at Father's jokes, so Father liked him," I said evasively, trying to sound encouraging.

"Your father's not going to have to live with him. What did he look like?"

I walked to the window and turned back to see a look of excitement in Bea's eyes. "He was cute, a little heavy, though."

She rose from her seat and came to stand beside me. She frowned. "He was fat?"

"His eyes were nice. I didn't really pay attention to him as I should have. You see, I had plans for that day with Master da Vinci."

"Master da Vinci? How is it you have plans with him?" Beatrice asked.

I smiled mischievously, and we exchanged excited glances. "Father had invited him to dinner, and I saw him later in the market." I placed a finger to my mouth so she knew to keep her voice down. "Bea, he has agreed to paint me," I whispered excitedly.

Bea looked puzzled for a moment. "Paint you?" she said with a sour look on her face.

"Quiet!" I hissed. "Do you want everyone to hear?"

"No, Lisa, this is not good," she said.

I knew Bea wouldn't understand. "He is a man of the world, a new thinker in art and science," I said defensively.

Bea was a friend, thinking of what's best for me, but she was not listening. "Bea you must listen—really listen. You are the only one I can truly talk to."

"Do you hear yourself? Think of what would happen if it were discovered that you let Master da Vinci paint you? Really, Lisa, you go too far."

I guess I should not have been surprised by her disapproval, but she chose to use this moment to remind me of my duty as the privileged daughter of a banker of Florence.

As she spoke, I read real concern for me in her eyes. For all her mischievous behavior Bea was a good friend.

"Well, anyway, after our guest left last night, I decided that I would not go through with it. But this morning . . ." I paused and looked away from her.

"This morning what?" She placed a hand on my thigh.

"I don't know, Bea. One minute I want to do it, the next I am having second thoughts. It all seemed so simple before. The nuns teach us we are to remain virtuous and beyond reproach before God. But does God not also care for our joy and the hope that we have for life?"

"Well, let me help you decide." Bea's golden hair fell forward as she leaned in to look eye to eye with me, her pretty face serious. "You are not going to do this," she said forcefully.

I sat there for a moment and thought carefully on what Beatrice had said. My logic on the subject seemed to elude me. What seemed so clear just a few days ago now sounded like foolishness, especially hearing it said aloud by Bea.

I hesitated for a moment and said, "No, I will not do it."

"You are sure of it, are you?" she asked.

"Yes, I am sure." I nodded my head slowly.

Chapter 5

That evening Father came in from a trip to the city, and although he seemed pleased to see me, for a brief few moments he could not look at me. Finally, he sat down and said, "Come and sit by me, my dear," patting the chair beside him. I sat and studied his face. I saw worry there. He seemed nervous and I began to feel uncomfortable. He reached out and took my hand. "I have arranged a match between you and Franco," he announced. "The marriage will take place in the spring of next year."

I stiffened at his words and withdrew my hand from his. Anger washed over me and tears appeared unbidden on my face at Father's betrayal. "I will not marry him," I protested. I stood to leave.

"You will. The matter has been decided."

"You promised me, Father. You promised that I could choose."

"We can't wait forever, darling."

"And why, Father? Because I am only a girl you must choose for me?"

His countenance softened, then, "Fathers choose for their daughters. This it is the way of it."

"Would you have broken your word to me if I had been a son and not a daughter?"

He bristled at the question. "Both of our families want this, my dear." His voice was now calm and controlled.

"What about what I want?"

"Please, for my sake, give the boy a chance. Get to know him and see if there is any hope for happiness."

"And if I find him unacceptable, will you call off the wedding?"

"It is unlikely, dear." There was a hint of indecision that suggested he was not sure. "Just give him a chance and I believe you will see what a fine young man he is."

"What does it matter? It seems I have little say," I said ruefully. I turned and stalked away, my steps echoing through the hall.

Later in my rooms I sat looking out the window. I was furious with Father. I could not believe he had agreed to this and without my permission. I was of a mind to elope with one of the neighborhood boys for spite, but then I would only prove myself an immature child.

I lay down on my bed and fell into an uneasy sleep. I awoke the next morning not wanting to even get out of bed, but it was Sunday and Father would be at my door wanting to know why I had not come down yet. I rose and dressed slowly. Not feeling like combing my hair, I pinned it back and wore a hat. I chose one of my old dresses and jacket and donned them without even brushing them. I went downstairs and immediately saw Father. I had not yet forgiven him and so did not speak to him when he said good morning. I behaved with ill grace while at the table for breakfast and politely refused to sit with him at church that morning, taking a place in the back of the church. In all, my behavior was reprehensible.

After the services were over, I was still withdrawn and in a contentious mood. Father didn't seem surprised when I chose to stay there rather than accompany him on his after church stroll through town. I sat looking at the prayer candles and was suddenly inspired to say a prayer myself. I lit a candle and knelt at the tiny altar. I thought of the week's events, of Signore da Vinci, of my betrothal to Franco and Father's betrayal.

As I knelt there, with my eyes closed, I felt the presence of someone standing behind me. I turned to see a priest. Startled, I began to rise.

"No, my child, don't get up. I didn't mean to disturb you." He was a big man with a wide face and a mass of ungovernable grey hair. He sat on the wooden bench near me with a grunt.

"I've not seen you here before, Reverend. Are you new to this church?" I asked.

"I am visiting here from the church in Careggi." His voice was as deep as his belly was wide.

"In Tuscany?" I said.

"You know of it?"

I nodded. "Only what my father has told me of the region."

"My name is Father Ficino. What is yours, my dear?"

"My name is Lisa. Pleased to meet you, Reverend."

He inclined his head at the introduction and his thick mane of grey hair tumbled forward into his face. "Are you alright, my dear?" he asked solicitously. "I saw you come in with your father and then noticed you chose not to sit with him during service, and you seemed, well, distressed."

"Nothing that an arranged marriage can't cure," I said.

"Ah, I see. And you don't love him?" He smoothed hair away from his face.

"I don't know him. I have only met him once. I mean, he seems nice, but . . ."

"But you do not love him, is this right?" I nodded in agreement. "Love is important, I agree," he said, "but it can also be a burden if he should break your heart. I prefer to see it as a privilege. You see, those whom we love are a gift to us because our care for them makes our lives rich and our hearts full."

"So I should accept this arrangement?" I asked.

"I am saying first we must see to our own hearts so we may love those whom God gives us."

"I don't understand." He had spoken words my heart needed to hear, but I remained unsure if I would be able to open my heart to another.

He placed a reassuring hand on my shoulder. "It is alright, you will in time. Please excuse me, my dear." With those words he stood to greet another parishioner.

I remained on my knees before the prayer altar, trying to piece together what he had meant. I was glad of his kindness, but I thought priests were supposed to speak in Latin, not in riddles. His words about the people we love being a gift had given me hope, but I didn't yet know what to do about it. I decided to walk home and think on it some more.

Chapter 6

When I returned home, I sat in the kitchen for a while, quietly watching the servants going about their work, until I noticed they were preparing trays with wine, cheese, and fruit. Just then Nelda came in to oversee the preparation and noticed me sitting there.

"There you are, signorina. Your lord father has requested you join him in the sala."

"Do we have guests here?" I asked.

"I believe it is your friend, Signorina Beatrice, and her mother." She returned her attention to the trays of food. I rose from my seat and stood there for a while to consider what a formal visit from Beatrice and her mother meant, for she had not mentioned it, and it was not like her mother to come unannounced.

I came in the door and three pairs of eyes turned to regard me. Beatrice was there with her mother, who stood behind her, arms crossed. Father turned last, standing by the fireplace.

"Come in here, Lisa," Father said. He shook his head in that distinct way he did when he was upset. "Your friend, Beatrice, has come to us with some disturbing news." Beatrice looked away as I entered. She sat at the table and stared into her hands folded in her lap.

Her mother eyed her with pursed lips and then reached out and prodded her. "Speak, child," she said harshly. Her mother was a slender woman with delicate features and, like Beatrice, she was fair-haired and tall. Beatrice had said she was cold and unaffectionate. She did have a fastidious way about her that was disciplined and unapproachable. Perhaps that was why Beatrice was so eager to please, sharing tidbits of intrigue or gossip as a way to make her feel wanted and needed.

Bea looked up at me and gave me a look of unease and agitation that I knew all too well. It was like we were little girls again and she had broken one of my dolls, but this time her face was laden with guilt and fear. "I told them of your plan with Master da Vinci," she whispered, her voice barely audible.

There was an awkward silence for a moment as I absorbed what Bea had just said. It was as if she had struck me in the presence of everyone in the room.

"And I promised I wouldn't go through with it," I said resentfully.

"I didn't believe you, Lisa, so I told Mother." She looked away from me, knowing she had betrayed me and broken our bond of trust in one another.

"How could you, Bea? I trusted you," I said through gritted teeth.

"That's enough, Lisa," Father said. "Sit down and explain yourself."

I sat, as Father bid me, but was reluctant to speak, for I found I was trembling with indignation.

"Like it or not, Beatrice did the right thing telling me," said Beatrice's mother. She walked towards me and stood in front of me with pursed lips and her arms still crossed, like she had been given charge over me. "And by sharing this with your father I had hoped to save your virtue, child. It seems being raised without a mother has left you, well, rather wanting for affection. Begging your pardon," she said, looking to Father.

Father frowned at her words but remained silent.

"You are like a sister to Beatrice," she continued. "So that makes you family. I would like you to come to me with anything, even just to chat." This she said while standing like a statue, pursed lips and all.

"Thank you, signora, but I would think you have enough to do with Beatrice."

"Your father and I have discussed this," she said, ignoring my insult.

I turned to Father and pointed at Beatrice's mother. "Is this where you got the idea to arrange my marriage? From her?"

Beatrice's mother rounded on me, her gown releasing the scent of jasmine as she stepped closer to me. "Your father didn't consult me about this arrangement, but it is for the best. An arrangement that you will ruin by allowing yourself to be painted like one of Duke Ludovico's mistresses, offering their sluttish wares to anyone who wants to see." She looked at me with disdain, as a woman who has thrown away the currency of her life on a foolish dream. Perhaps she was right, but her words still offended me.

"She has done nothing," Father protested with annoyance.

She turned towards Father. "Yes, but if she poses for a man who has captured the likeness of every mistress the Duke of Milan has fancied, who will believe in her innocence?" Then she glanced towards me. "You must accept that we know what is best for you."

"Really. And you would know what is best for me," I shouted. I could feel my heart pounding and my hands were shaking. "Well, I would rather die than come to speak to you!"

"Lisa!" Father shouted. "You will apologize."

I looked to Father and then to Beatrice, who was no longer engaged in the conversation. She just sat there, hair disheveled and eyes cast down.

In response, I turned and swept out through the same door I had come in and into the via in front of our house.

The sky was a curtain of slate blue with angry clouds gathering in the summer day.

I looked up into the gale swept sky as heavy rain began to fall, soaking me, ruining my dress, and fueling my indignation, and I wished I had thought to bring a hat or overcoat. Not knowing what to do, I walked around the city aimlessly for several hours.

Beatrice's mother's words were terse and harsh. She had left me angry as she had meant to.

I no doubt showed her what she had wanted to see in me. That I was quarrelsome and rebellious. Which meant I was incapable of making my own decisions. I had taken the bait and given her just what she wanted and gotten upset.

Of all things, Bea's betrayal hurt the most. She was my friend, sharing everything with me. Yes, she was a gossip, but I thought she cared about me. I didn't understand why she would do this. What I did know is that no one was going to tell me what was best for me—not Father, who had broken his promise to me, and certainly not Bea's mother.

The rain had stopped and the sky was clearing. I walked the Piazza Della Signoria that was always filled with painters and artisans ever since Lord Medici called the artisans of Italy to come to Florence. It had become a place where artists displayed their work. There were beautiful paintings, drawings, and sculptures being sold. I watched as a young painter set up his easel and canvas and began to paint in the midst of the trees in the Piazza, the water still dripping from their leaves. Although no one seemed to take notice of him, his face was lit with passion and contentment.

It was then I began thinking of my situation again. Father could try to arrange my life, Beatrice and her mother could try to preserve my virtue for the customs or conventions of Florence, but was it really wrong to long for love and beauty? If they thought allowing myself to be captured in a beautiful work of art to be sinful, then it was their failing, not mine. Suddenly it was clear what I had to do. All my circumspection and restraint fell away. My desire to be true to myself was stronger. I did not have to reawaken it. It was there waiting just beneath the surface, waiting for me to say yes, I would do it.

"Yes," I said aloud.

The young painter looked up and smiled. Perhaps he thought I was complimenting his work.

"Excuse me, signore," I said. He returned to his work without another look towards me, but I thought of him and his simple joy all the way home.

The next morning at breakfast I knew Father would insist on talking about my behavior. I spoke little, as Father expected, barely acknowledging his presence at table.

"She meant well, you know," Father said, weakly defending Beatrice's mother. "You spoke rashly and without thought, Lisa, and you will have to apologize to Beatrice's mother."

I knew he would bring up my conduct towards Bea's mother. But I was in no mood to appease Father.

"Serves her right. She provoked me on purpose."

"We don't speak to people disrespectfully."

"She earned my disrespect, Father. You heard her."

He sighed. "Maybe I have coddled you, and since your mother has been gone, perhaps you do lack something. I don't know."

"Yes, Father, I *have* truly lacked something." Desire, passion, perhaps self-respect, but I reasoned he would think I meant the lack of a mother.

Father opened his mouth to speak but I placed a hand on his shoulder. "You are right, Father. It is my problem to work out, and I will."

With those words I stood and left.

Chapter 7

I went to the address Master da Vinci had written in his letter, the old Servite monastery of Santissima in the older part of the city. The door was open.

A woman in a faded tunic and white apron sat at a table eating. She stood and brushed crumbs from her dress as I entered. I gave her the parchment da Vinci had given me. She glanced at it and tossed it among the remains of her breakfast.

"Master da Vinci is not here," she said. "He has been called away for a few days. Come back another day." She began closing the door without so much as even looking at me again.

"Wait," I said, putting my foot firmly in the doorway. "When will he return?"

She blinked for a moment and looked down at my foot. Her eyes rose from my obstinate foot until she leveled on my eyes. "You're going to lose that foot if you don't move it."

"Just tell me when he will return, and I will leave."

She glowered at me for a moment and then said, "Sunday. He will return on Sunday."

I removed my foot, and she slammed the door.

The next day I went to the monastery for my devotional instruction. As I entered the room Bea was already there amid the clatter of girls. I didn't sit in my regular seat. Instead, I chose a seat on the other side of the room, opposite Bea. She didn't look at me when I came in the room, and I sensed she was trying to ignore me. I looked at her and for a moment she looked dark and menacing, threatening even, but then maybe it was the light. Later I looked back at her again and decided it was the light.

After our studies were finished Bea came over and gave me some fruit from her garden—cherries, my favorite. Of course, she knew this, and my guess was she had given me a peace offering. I accepted but said nothing. This repeated for two more days. Each time she spoke to me, I said little besides a grunt to acknowledge I was not deaf.

Finally, Bea could take no more. "How long are you going to stay mad at me?" she said, pushing the fruit she had brought into my hand. "I had no idea Mother was going to go to your father." She took hold of one of my hands.

I pulled away. "What does that matter? You should not have told her."

"I was worried. You sounded like you were going to do something really crazy."

I could feel myself begin to tremble at the thought of what her next words would be. "What else have you told your mother? I couldn't bear the thought of her knowing anything more of my affairs."

"She only wanted to protect you. Is that so bad?"

"Protect me from what?"

"From yourself. You said it yourself; you were confused."

"I don't want her help." I turned away from her, thinking I had heard quite enough.

She walked around my chair to face me. "Lisa, I don't think you know what you want."

I was saddened at her words because, of all the people in my life, I expected Bea to be among the ones who understood me. "And you and your mother do?" I rose from my chair. "Stay away from me, Bea." I shoved the fruit back at her and walked away.

"Lisa, wait," she called.

But I didn't look back.

That same month Franco's family met with Father and agreed to terms. Our stewards met, and an agreement was written up by our lawyers. We were to be married in the spring. It was an agreement without passion—no betrothal with offerings of love or affection, just a cold contract of obligation and efficiency. I was fifteen years old, and he was an old man to me of thirty. I was starting to believe my worst fears were coming to pass.

The next day Nelda announced the arrival of Franco and his parents who had come to formalize the arrangement of our betrothal. She returned to my rooms to cheerfully fuss over the preparation of my hair and the laying out of my dress, the bodice with the cioppa overgown. She was full of approbation about my beautiful hair and skin, for she had served my mother and often reminded me of how much like her I was.

Father summoned me to our sala where I found him seated with Franco and his mother, with Franco's father standing beside his wife's chair.

As I entered, they looked me up and down like a horse they might buy. Father bade me sit. "May I present my daughter, Signorina Lisa." Father began bowing in my direction. I rose from my chair and offered a deep curtsy at the introduction. "And these are Franco's parents, Signore Bartolomeo and Signora Camilla del Giocondo." They both inclined their heads and offered me pleasant smiles while their eyes examined me.

"You are welcome in our home," I said with practiced formality, repeating the expected greeting.

Franco's father was thin and short with a bald head half hidden under a rich woolen cap. His wife was taller than him and I could see where Franco had inherited his gray eyes and blond hair.

Franco's mother hesitated for a moment, glanced over at Father and me, and then began. "May I speak forthrightly, dear?" she said, looking directly at me. Father agreed for the both of us and so prevented my refusal. "As you know, your father and my husband and I have arranged a match between you and our son Franco. We hope that you will consider this a most advantageous offer. In short, we are very much in agreement on you and Franco."

Although I already knew of this arrangement, I said nothing in response.

"A great honor this," Father said agreeably. "A great match for them both."

"Do you have something you wish to say, dear?" Signora del Giocondo asked, her voice suddenly warm as she saw my hesitancy.

"Yes, of course . . . a great honor," I said feebly, trying to sound confident, but my voice was thin and indifferent.

She ignored my reluctance. "You will come to me with any of your concerns, dear," she insisted and turned to her husband. He inclined his head in agreement.

"Well, now, it is settled," Franco's father observed, a wide grin on his face.

I offered a deep curtsy of respect in acknowledgment of the formal betrothal between our two families, as was the custom. But in my heart there was a growing resentment toward these people that I hardly knew.

While our families discussed the arrangement of the ceremony, Franco and I sat there together like two sacrificial lambs.

"I have no need of a husband right now," I said softly so only he could hear. Franco remained silent. "It is my father who insists that it is in my best interests to marry you," I said coldly, "but I assure you it is not what I have dreamed."

He looked over at me with pity in his eyes. "I see you have made up your mind," he said finally. "What is your dream? Help me understand."

"To live a full life, to see the world and explore its beauty, to fall in love with someone I adore and who adores me . . . not some arranged marriage."

He turned to me and took my hand in his. "Lisa, you must know you could never choose your own life. You are a girl, after all, and girls have no choice." I bristled at his words. "But as your husband I can give you this choice. And I will respect your wishes in every way."

I felt anger rising in me. "So you would have me as nothing more than a brood cow for you? Birthing your children without the presence of affection?" I was watching him so I might weigh his response to my provocation, knowing that this man Father had selected for me should be my husband and his opinions mine to honor.

But he leaned closer and looked into my eyes and I saw ease and warmth in his face where I expected to see rejection and anger. "Since you want nothing to do with me and somehow find me unsuitable," he smiled then, "perhaps an arrangement that is binding but unconsummated would suit us both equally," he said cheerfully.

For a moment I wondered if there could be such an arrangement where he could be my husband and never share my bed. I quickly dismissed the idea, for I saw I could not anger him.

I stood and swept to the door and placed my hand on the latch. But I had second thoughts about leaving without a word of courtesy to Father or to Franco's family. I turned and noticed all eyes in the room were upon me and Franco had followed me to the door and stood beside me. He leaned in so close I could feel the warmth of his breath on my cheek.

"I know this arrangement is not how you envisioned your marriage," he said in a small voice, "or even for your life. But do you really want to argue with me when I'm prepared to give you all that your heart desires?"

I looked into his eyes then to measure the meaning of this dutiful son mouthing words that I believed were influenced by his parents. "I don't know, signore," I said stubbornly. "Why should I believe you to be sincere or honorable?" I was no longer able to keep the anger from my voice.

He heard the anger in my voice and stepped back from me. He studied my face for a moment and bowed. "Good night, signorina."

I glanced over Franco's shoulder towards his parents and Father and saw the aghast look on their faces at my behavior. I turned and left the room. I heard Father apologizing for my behavior and suggesting they should let Franco and me work things out.

After dinner, as we sat reading by the fire, I pulled my chair closer to Father so our servants could not hear. "Do you remember what you said when it came time for me to marry?" I asked.

He looked away as though he would avoid this conversation. "I remember, dear," he said wearily.

"All those years you promised, you said there would be an exception for me."

"And I know now that I was wrong to promise it." He closed the book he was reading and turned to me. "You have cause for complaint for what I have done," he said softly, "but this is the world you have been born into, my dear, and there can be no exception for you. You have been allowed to dream, but now that time is over. Now you must grow up and accept your duty to marry the man who has been chosen for you for the honor of our house."

"You said you wanted me to live the life that Mother could not." Father flinched at the mention of Mother, the woman he loved, the woman who broke his heart when she was taken from him, buried in silence all these years. "You promised me that the life that was taken from her would continue in me, so that in me a part of her could live."

He listened patiently and nodded as though he was considering what I was saying. He walked to the window looking out over the evening sky, and he glanced at me as if he was weighing the moment. "Your mother died giving birth to you," he said softly. "Lucrezia was the love of my life." Father swallowed hard after mentioning her name and was lost for a moment in his grief.

I saw how Father had carried the weight of this guilt, and I had been recklessly throwing her name around without understanding what she meant to him. I paused to absorb what he said and realized that I was a fool for using her memory to get my way.

Father came back and sank into his chair next to me. "She was dearly loved by me. It was our dream of having children," he said, "dreams of you and other children that we would have that were the cause of her death." His eyes filled with tears.

"You mustn't blame yourself, Father." I wanted to remain angry with him, but he had melted my resolve with his tears. "I believe Mother would want your memories of her to be of what you had, not what you lost. You know full well women face the risk of childbirth willingly as the price to bring children into a family." As I said these words I knew they were more for me than for Father, for I could not see beyond the hope and dreams I had.

"Then it is a cruel price," said Father. We sat quietly for a while watching the fire.

"I know you are right," he said calmly. "And I know your mother would be proud of you. But you must decide whether you are a child or a woman so you can manage your own affairs."

I smiled at his encouragement but said nothing, for I had more to say but didn't think Father could hear it now.

In truth, I felt as though a great shadow had fallen over my hopes and dreams, and that I had to accept my place as a wife and pledge myself to Franco and become flesh of his flesh and bone of his bone in holy matrimony.

The next day I went to the Mercato Vecchio, but with Adriana, one of the girls who also attended the monastery. She was short and stubby with light brown curly hair and a friend to Bea and me. She saw we weren't speaking and didn't bother to ask why. She was kind of self-involved and snobbish, for her family had one of the oldest and largest banks in the city, and that meant she considered herself above the rest of us. She often spoke of the royal parties her family attended. Adriana fully expected to be betrothed to the son of some wealthy lord or baron.

"You will wait here while I look at these wares," she said to her servants, although she seemed to be looking at me like she couldn't tell the difference.

"You go on. I will sit awhile by the fountain," I said lightly, hoping she would decide not to join me. She was nice but she and Bea got on better than we did, and I liked her best when Bea was around.

"I won't be long," she said.

I sat in my favorite spot and rested my head on the cool stones. I was enjoying the sun and the soft sounds of the fountain when I heard his voice.

"I thought you had been truly interested in sitting for me." I turned to see Master da Vinci standing there. "But then you didn't show up." He said the words not as a provocation, but as a puzzle he had to solve. "And then you came to my home and showed my letter of invitation."

I began to speak but he raised a hand to signify he wasn't finished talking. "So one could assume," he continued, "that you have changed your mind, but why? What has changed for you that caused you not to seek me out?" He turned his head towards me with an expectant look on his face, waiting upon my answer.

"Truth is . . . I lost my nerve, signore," I began hesitantly, for I was reluctant to share my indecision with him. This great man of the new learning, who had invited me to be part of his world, should not be told I was bound by the conventions and traditions of old.

"You were not certain before?"

"I thought I was."

"And now?"

"I want this."

He paused for a moment, thoughtfully considering the look of desire upon my face. "Why? Why now?" He inclined his head slightly as though he had asked the question to himself.

"Does it matter?" I protested.

"Sometimes the reason behind creative expression is the most important question. So you see, it is of great importance to me."

I hesitated.

"Perhaps another time then." He turned to walk away.

I rose to my feet and called after him. "I want to be part of something beautiful . . . something that is mine. I believe you can do this . . . show me as I truly am, I mean."

He turned around to regard me. He seemed unmoved by my confession for a moment. Then a smile formed on his face.

Chapter 8

The next day was a Saturday, and I returned to Master da Vinci's place early in the morning. The same woman who had spoken to me before was there. She nodded at my greeting and held out her hand to take my coat. She had this pained expression on her face. "You can go in. Remove your clothes and the master will be along in a moment."

"Excuse me," I said. "There must be some mistake. Master da Vinci said nothing of removing my clothes."

"You have been paid, haven't you?"

I could feel my heart pounding. "I will not be insulted."

She smiled at my insolence. "You're not the first one to sit for Master da Vinci. I know what you are," she sneered.

"Maria, that will be enough," a voice said. I turned to see Signore da Vinci standing in the doorway. "That will be all for today, signora," he said. Maria gathered her belongings and strode past da Vinci as though she had been insulted instead of me.

"My apologies for her behavior," he said. "She mistook you for one of the young ladies who sit for me so that I may practice my craft. Truly she meant nothing by it."

"She was quite clear about what she meant," I said, suddenly feeling like I should not have come.

He took my hand. I was startled because he had never touched me before.

"Follow me," he said in a soft voice. I meekly followed him. We went through a dark hallway that opened to a large room with a high ceiling and exposed cross beams. It appeared to be a storage building of some sort, for half of the room was filled with farm equipment, while the other half was empty save for a low platform with a padded chair, easel, and several rows of paintings leaning against the wall.

"This workshop was owned by my old teacher, Signore Verrocchio. I spent many years working in this very room."

At first glance his workspace seemed to be a cluttered jumble of paint brushes, palettes, and jars of tints and pigments, but later when I saw him work I observed there was a symmetry to the arrangement of everything there.

His workshop was on the grounds of the monastery, in one of the outbuildings overlooking the pasture. It was simple with a beautiful view of the river.

"It is quaint," I said quietly, suddenly feeling out of place and overwhelmed with the idea of posing for Master da

Vinci. What did he expect of me? What if he no longer found me interesting?

Master da Vinci picked up a wooden stool from amid the clutter of his workshop and sat in front of his easel. "Sit," he commanded, pointing toward the padded chair. His voice was calm and reassuring. I sat down and began to speak but he waved me to silence while he studied me with thoughtful pleasure, his eyes surveying every inch of me for what seemed a long time. Something changed in his face, for he looked at me critically for a moment, then he abruptly stood up.

"No, it's all wrong." He walked over to one of the wide doors that led to the outside and flung it open. Bright sunlight flooded in turning my hair and clothes to golden hues of auburn and amber.

"Perfect," he said quietly.

He lifted his easel and arranged it so the sunlight was behind me and then I saw that smile again. This intrigued me. I wanted to know more about his craft and his approach to painting. I tried to ask questions of him, but he placed a paint covered finger to his lips and said, "Shhh. Be in the moment, my dear."

Concentration settled over his bearded face as he painted, and in long intervals his eyes would meet mine and, not meaning to, I would *smile*.

After many hours of working, he paused and turned the painting so that I might see it. What I saw took my breath away. It was a masterpiece. He had transformed the weary hours of sitting in tedium and boredom into a work of divine inspiration. It had been elegantly painted, each lightness and darkness perfectly rendered. Every curve and detail carefully captured. The woman that stared back at me was beautiful, possessing a poise I did not think I had. Her hands were crossed, and she looked through me as if in contemplation of some secret amusement. I was speechless in admiration for a moment, quietly taking in the beauty before me.

"Are you pleased?" He chuckled, delighted at my reaction to his work.

"Yes, yes, it is truly wonderful," I breathed. "Is it truly as you see me, signore?" I turned to look at him, my face brimming with pleasure. The corner of his mouth arced into a wide grin I had never before seen on his face.

"Yes, it is you, my dear. All you." But even as he spoke there was a distant ache. A foreboding. Although the painting had pleased me, I could not shake the feeling that after all my resolve to do things my own way, I knew on some level that what I had done would be grievous to Father. It overshadowed my enjoyment of what Master da Vinci had created and made what was sweet . . . bittersweet.

The sun was setting, and the evening shadows lengthened. He shut the wide doors of his workspace and began putting away brushes and paint pots. I was tired of posing for Master da Vinci and thought I should be getting home before I would be missed.

"When will it be finished?" I asked.

"There is still much work needed for the background of the painting and to bring out more of your beauty," he said with a faint smile.

I returned a smile, not yet used to hearing of my newfound beauty, and turned my attention to the stacks of paintings that leaned against the walls. "What will you do with it?" I asked. It occurred to me I had never asked this of him. I had only thought to pose, not to ask about what he would do with the painting. I imagined it would be part of his collection. I had never seen paintings of his other subjects and assumed they were a confidential matter, that he would exercise the same discretion I observed he had for the privacy of the royal family. But this was not to be so, because he had known all along what he would do with it.

He leaned forward from his stool. "I will display my work at Lady Alfonsina Medici's birthday celebration ball this month," he announced. "As you know, the Medici family are patrons of sorts to many artisans and creative thinkers in Florence. Several of them will also display their work." He placed a hand on my shoulder. "My painting of you is a special work indeed. I have truly made you immortal. You will be the envy of all, you will see."

This silenced me completely. I bit my tongue on the reproach that I believed our work together would be a thing of secrecy and confidence. Though I had little interest in his reasons I didn't have the courage to object.

I searched his face for a moment. It was flush with the exaltation of our shared joy of his creation. I did not know what to make of his announcement to exhibit the painting. So I said my farewells and began my walk home.

My mind was racing at the prospect of what he had said. I had not considered the weight of my decision until I understood I was to be placed on display for all to see. And the elixir of my passion to explore beauty had begun to wear off, for it would seem the consequences of my decision to defy Father were coming back faster than I expected. All my desire to be released from the constraints of the careful behavior of a daughter of privilege and nobility had been replaced by a rising fear that I would be a great source of shame and disgrace for Father.

Chapter 9

On Sunday I was to accompany Father to church at Santa Trinita. As we were riding in the carriage Father began to talk about the scandal surrounding Master da Vinci, and the painting of the duke's mistress Cecilia Gallerani, and of the numerous young ladies he had painted.

"Some of them were from the finest of families," Father said.

"And what of the men who pay for them to be painted? Do they not share in this scandal, Father?"

"It is the way of things," he said. "Many people talk of the new times we live in, of art and science. But some things have not changed, my dear. Surely no one would want to marry a woman who would allow herself to be degraded in such a way."

I thought of Cecilia Gallerani who was now a nobody—having no place or fortune after the fall of the duke and named as a whore by everyone—with no one to take her in. "I think you're wrong, Father." But I knew there was some truth in what he had said. I could not shake a growing feeling of guilt, that I had done something wrong.

Father and I rode the rest of the way to church in stony silence. He saw I was upset and so said nothing. I turned my head away from him and looked out over the greening meadows and golden wheat fields that were ablaze in the sunlight as we crossed over the San Niccolò bridge. None of its beauty gave me comfort or pleasure.

I looked over at Father again, who was now reading one of his books, and as I turned away, out of the corner of my eye I saw him looking up at me and shaking his head at my downcast behavior.

I sat lost in my thoughts. How could something I had wanted so badly become such a great mess of my own making? I remembered the excitement of my time with Master da Vinci and the passion so powerful it filled me with joy.

But now it seemed a distant memory of a joy far off and lost from me.

By the time our carriage pulled up to the church my eyes were tearing up. During the church service I didn't remember the hymnals or the reverend's sermon and it was soon over.

"Come, my dear," Father said, standing.

"I want to stay for a while," I said, wanting to sit in the quiet of the church after mass was finished to think about what I had done . . . maybe even to pray if God would listen.

"Are you alright?" Father asked.

I nodded, looking away from him, not wanting to meet his observant gaze.

"Very well, I will be back in an hour," he said, putting on his hat.

After Father left, I lingered in the cool of the church. The empty eye sockets of the statue of Christ stared back at me with unseeing eyes, but I felt he knew of my sin. The gloom of the church was almost comforting, hiding me from the shame of what I had done with Master da Vinci. The weight of my guilt rested heavily upon me as the nuns at Santa Trinita said it would. And my mind was beset with a foreboding worry of the sin of disobedience against Father that endangered my mortal soul to purgatory or worse. I feared that what I had done with Master da Vinci had moved me towards it.

"Why are you here, child?" a voice said.

I looked up to see Father Ficino standing above me with concern upon his wide face. At first I said nothing, hoping my silence would cause him to go away and leave me to my thoughts, but my eyes filled with tears again and I turned away from him. He just quietly sat next to me, and after a few moments we fell into a companionable silence.

Finally, I whispered, "Reverend, is it sinful to dream of things we know are wrong, even if we do not do them?" The priest remained silent. Only the clip-clop of a passing horse and carriage could be heard. "I am a woman now," I continued, "and a woman wants to be admired for her beauty." I paused for a moment, uncertain if I should continue. "The painter . . . he made me immortal," I said, turning again to look at the priest. I told him the whole story of Master da Vinci, how Father had forbidden me to allow myself to be painted, and how I had defied him.

"So then have I sinned, Reverend?"

He leaned forward, took my hand, and spoke softly, his deep voice a low rumble. "In dishonoring your father, yes." He paused for a moment. "But in allowing yourself to be painted, I cannot say." He drew close so his voice would not disturb other parishioners praying in the church. "When our hearts are alive God is pleased." He turned to look into my eyes, and I could smell his breakfast of cheese and onion on his breath. "When you were being painted was your heart alive?"

"Yes. Yes, Reverend."

"Then there can be no sin in it, child." He patted my hand. "But there is the matter of your father and your heart toward him. You see, Christ made sin exceedingly more sinful. For Christ taught us that sin begins first within us, in our hearts and in our thoughts and finally in our actions, but then so does His immense love and forgiveness."

Father Ficino spoke for a long time that day, and I don't remember all his words, but they were life. I drank them in like a parched field in Tuscany before the spring rains. I saw that I had again behaved like a child, thinking of my own desires and not of Father, and how hard it had been for him to raise me on his own without Mother. I decided my need for the painting was not more important than my need to honor Father. I would go to Master da Vinci and ask him to remove the painting from exhibit and put this behind us.

Chapter 10

I stood outside his door for an hour. It began to rain, something for which I was grateful so Master da Vinci would not see that I had been crying. I closed my eyes for a moment and when all I could hear was rain falling, I wished the rainstorm could last for days, causing the river to rise above the banks and flood the city and save me from my shame. But it would not be so. Even though I had spent most of the day praying to God for an answer, I opened my eyes as the pattering sound of rain softened and the sun began to peek through the grey skies.

Signore da Vinci finally came walking around the corner. I recognized his loping stride from far away. He greeted me and invited me in out of the rainswept street. I followed him into the workshop where I had sat for him.

He was in a cheerful mood, humming as he moved about. He asked me to sit and poured some cider. My painting was still on his easel among the blank canvases, paint pots, and brushes. I looked at it ruefully now that it represented my willful disobedience of Father, and though only my face, hands, and bodice had been completed, I was lost in its simple beauty for a moment.

"What is it, my dear?" he said, waking me from my trance. "Is something wrong?"

At first I said nothing, for I didn't know where to begin. How I could tell this man, that I had begged to paint me, that I had changed my mind . . . again.

"Father thinks it was a mistake to let you paint me," I blurted out finally. I lied, for Father knew nothing of my adventure with Master da Vinci. "He believes it will make me unsuitable for marriage should anyone learn of it." I spoke for a long time, of my conversations with Father and with the priest at the church. I poured my heart out to him, but he just looked at me as though he were still painting me. His eyes flowed over me like he was considering some aspect of my face that he might capture.

Frustrated, I took hold of his arm and shook him. "Did you hear me? I want you to not show the painting."

His eyes found mine. "Yes, I understand," he said irritably, pulling away from me. "But no, no, my dear, I think I will keep it in the exhibit."

Cold slid down my spine as I realized what he was saying. I was so shocked that I stood for a moment with my mouth hung open. I tried to hide my indignation because I had been raised with a banker's daughter's pride.

I could not help but hear Father's words ringing out in my head—that things had really not changed, and no one would want me if it were discovered I had degraded myself. I could see Bea shaking her head in disgust, and Franco . . . would even Franco want me once he had heard what I had done? What had I been thinking? I could feel my heart pounding as these thoughts raced through my mind. Finally, I could take no more.

"Please. Please," I begged. The words felt strange in my mouth. Begging wasn't something I had ever done before. "For my honor, signore, do not show the painting. No one need see it."

He had turned away from me as though he would rather not look upon the desperation on my face. So I stepped closer to him and placed a hand on his shoulder. "Don't you understand, signore," I said, trying to calm myself. "If you show it, if you show me to all of Florence, it will bring shame to my family and to my father. You see, he has arranged a match between me and the son of another family. When they hear of my indiscretion, Father will be ridiculed, and I will be deemed unsuitable for marriage. Surely you have heard the rumors about the girls you have painted, heard how they are regarded by the people who discover what they have done. If it were to be revealed I allowed you to paint me, the same rumors would circulate about me. Have you no pity, no care for my honor, signore?"

In answer to my show of emotion he turned to look at me but did not speak for a moment. He sat looking at me quietly, and I at him, with all the pleading I could summon upon my face.

After a time, he spoke into the silence. "This is your opportunity for timelessness, my dear," he said evenly. "Your beauty will stand for all time. I thought that's what you wanted?"

I looked at him blankly. His words no longer stirred me, for I had seen his true nature. Yes, brilliance was there, ingenuity, and even genius. But there was also indifference and self-serving ambition.

Chapter 11

I saw no other way, no other alternative before me. I would have to tell Father, and I truly feared what this might do to him.

When I arrived home Father sat in his chair reading as he always did before dinner. He looked up as I entered the room and I paused and looked uncertainly toward him for a moment, wondering if I should go through with it.

"What is it, my dear?" Father said absently, absorbed over his books of accounts.

"I sat for Master da Vinci," I began in a small voice.

"What?" he said, distracted by my words.

I looked around the room, wishing I could keep it a secret just a little longer. "I sat for Master da Vinci," I repeated numbly. "I allowed him to paint me."

Father did not speak for a moment. His face twisted into a look of honest confusion. "You allowed yourself to be painted?" He stood. "Lisa, what have you done, child? You ask to make your own choices, and this is what you have chosen?" he shouted. His body shook with anger.

"Father, if you would but look at the painting you would see its beauty; you would see it was done with care and much respect."

He looked at me for a moment, his face suffused with disappointment. "I will hear no more of this today," he said. With this he turned and stalked out of the room, and I heard him slam the door of his study. I was disoriented for a moment not knowing what to make of Father's abrupt behavior. He had not lectured me as was his normal way, nor did he give out a punishment or order me to my room. Perhaps he was struggling with how to relate to a young woman, and not a little girl. This was new ground for us both and, admittedly, I was as unsure as he was on how to conduct myself.

I went out into my garden and worked in the soil in the cool of the evening. It was my place of solitude, where I could think, on my knees cultivating my plants, the only thing I seemed to have control of. I had been there only a few minutes when I saw the silhouette of someone sitting on the stone bench. I turned to see Franco and he was smiling at me. No doubt he expected me to come into the garden.

He glanced at the servant working on the other side of the garden. "Is it true?" he said breathlessly.

I avoided his question. "How long have you been sitting there?"

"I was in the house."

"Oh, I see."

"Long enough to hear you and your father. The walls in the old villa are not so thick. I think all of your servants heard your words."

I turned to gather the clay pots used for seedlings and I heard him stand and walk closer. He bent down. "Let me be of service, signorina," he said with a shrug of his shoulders.

"And why . . . why would you help me? Didn't you and your family get what they wanted from this arranged marriage?" I chided. "As I remember it, you were very clear about what you wanted. Why risk further disfavor by helping me?"

He offered a warm smile in answer. "But weren't you also, though?" he said. "Weren't you quite clear about what you wanted? You told me that you had no need of a husband, that this marriage was only to appease your father and that you wished to live your life on your own terms and marry whom you chose and fell in love with."

He was right, of course, for I had said that and more. Surely he knew love was not a requirement in our arranged marriage. But maybe I wanted him to at least try to kindle an affection for me.

"Since you have no desire one way or the other for me, the least you could do is stay out of my affairs and let me handle this my own way," I said.

He leaned in closer to me. "Yes, it is true, I was told there was no need of affection, that you brought a family name and wealth. And while I accepted this, I had hoped that in time there would be," he paused for a moment, "that you would come to care for me and perhaps someday . . ." He broke off and smiled again and sat beside me on the ground. "I still believe I could be of service to you," he said in a soft voice so as not to be overheard by anyone in the Villa.

"And just how could you do that?" I said, looking into his grey eyes.

"It seems you find yourself in a difficult circumstance that is beyond you and perhaps I can help."

"Yes, but how?"

"I have a plan, but I think it best I do not say."

I sighed in desperation. "Franco, this is not the time for a show of empty chivalry. I am in real trouble."

His eyes searched my face for a time and then he said, "What is the painting like?

I looked away. "It is pleasing . . . beautiful even, I guess, but that is not the point."

"Isn't it?" he asked. "Isn't it why you risk so much?" I began to speak but he took my hand and spoke. "I have seen your face in my dreams. I need no painting to convince me of your beauty. I would protect your honor, signorina."

"And why would you do this for me after how I behaved?"

"Isn't it obvious?" he said. He smiled again and stood. "Think about my offer of service to you, signorina." He offered a deep bow and departed.

What was obvious? I reasoned. The question hung in my mind, and I thought on his words for the rest of the night.

Chapter 12

I went to bed that night still worried, but at least there was hope in Franco's offer to support me. I recalled the glint in his eyes and the warmth of his smile and when I thought on his words "isn't it obvious?" I blushed and my heart was made glad at the memory of it.

A few days later I saw him again at our house with Father and he smiled at me with his grey eyes and blond easy charm, and for a moment I didn't know what to think of it.

He was standing there in his leather riding boots with fine wool trousers and a rich cloth doublet of gold and his riding cloak slung over his shoulder.

My heart beat a little faster at the sight of him.

And when he had a moment away from Father's attention he came into our sala where I was and sat beside me.

"Have you thought about our talk?" he asked.

Every moment I have been away from you, I thought. "Yes," I said. And smiled at his question, but I was smiling so wide I had to look away for a moment out of embarrassment.

He saw my smile and returned a warm grin. "And you . . . would like me to be your champion? And pledge myself to your defense and safety?" he said playfully.

I nodded and I giggled and remarked how good it felt to laugh in the middle of my troubles.

He leaned in close, his face suddenly serious. "I will speak with my father," he whispered, his breath warm on my neck. "He has influence in Milan with the governor appointed by King Louis of France. Perhaps he can arrange for Master da Vinci to show his painting there where no one would know you. At the very least, I will speak to my father to see if he can inquire about the painting to purchase it."

I heard his words and observed the sincerity on his face and put my hand on his to silence him. In response, he gently covered my hand with his own and for a moment we were handclasped like close friends, and for the first time I realized I was thinking of him as more than a stranger that had been forced upon me in marriage. He gently drew me towards him and put his arm around me. I flushed with desire at his touch as he held me close enough to smell the musk of his hair. And I felt myself relax into the comfort of his arms.

"Why would your father want a painting of me?" I said apprehensively.

He looked thoughtful for a moment. "So that we may protect your honor," he said quietly. "I will send word to my father immediately," he vowed.

A smile erupted on my face.

Over the next few days, Franco showed his affection for me, not with words or making a fuss over me, but in the simple things like quietly working beside me in the garden, or bringing me my meals from the kitchen to ensure I was served first, before he got his meals. And sharing of his childhood with me as the son of a merchant and councilman of the city of Florence. How he wanted to be a great knight and condottiero like the great military commanders of Italy. But his father had sent him away to school to empty him of these ambitions. In return, I told him of my secret adventures with Bea in the Mercato Vecchio and of my interest in the new learning of science, sculpture, and painting like the masters Donatello, da Vinci, and Michelangelo. And he laughed out loud when I said maybe someday I would create beauty as they do. Then, not wanting to offend me, he stifled his laughter and grew quiet.

I smiled at him, observing his tender care of my feelings. "Are you fearful a girl could not take part in the new learning, signore?" I said mischievously and he beamed back a smile, relieved I had not taken offense.

Then he leaned back to look at me and I could not resist the temptation to look into his grey eyes. I could feel the color rising in my face, but I could not take my eyes from his. He leaned forward and kissed me. I pulled away from him breathlessly, and his smiling upward glance told me he shared my passion. I thought of his kiss for the rest of the day and began to understand what the ache of desire feels like.

A few days later at the monastery, no sooner had I sat at my seat than Bea was standing over me, her arms crossed in the same mannerism of her mother. Her posture suggested she was displeased.

I ignored her for a while and then, finally, I looked up at her.

"It seems our friend, Adriana, and her family are patrons of the arts here in the city and they have been visiting some of the artists to view their work in the hope of buying before everyone else," she said.

What should I care about Adriana and her family's interest in art? She was really Bea's friend and not mine. "So what business is this of mine?" I said.

"When they visited Master da Vinci . . ." she paused.

"When they visited Master da Vinci what?" I prompted.

She inclined her head like a curious bird and studied me for a while. "There is a painting there that Adriana says looks a lot like you."

Her words drove the breath from me, and for a moment I could not speak. I turned my attention from Bea and stared out the window, visibly shaken by her words.

"Please, Lisa, please tell me it is not you." But the look on my face was all she needed to know she had been right.

"Are you so much the fool that you don't know what you have done?" she said.

"I only wanted to be beautiful, Bea, but look what a mess I have made." My eyes welled up with tears.

"Tell me why, Lisa? Was your life so unbearable that you had to bring humiliation to your family?" She was right, but I could only nod my head while tears flowed.

"Now what will you do? Is there any suitor now that would even have you?"

"I have tried to get Master da Vinci not to show the painting. I have begged, petitioned, and prayed to God but no amount of supplication has worked." Bea's countenance had changed now from disappointment to pity, but she just stood there looking at me.

"What can I do?" I said, turning to her. Bea sat down next to me and placed a hand on mine. I told her the whole story of how Master da Vinci had painted me, of his plans to exhibit the painting before all of Florence, and even of Franco's plan to help me.

"We will think of something, Lisa." She spoke her words evenly and calmly with no reproach, not wanting to cause me further anguish

"Is there anything that can be done?" I said, looking up into Bea's eyes. I knew the answer before I asked the question—there was nothing I could do. Franco had promised to help but it seemed he might not be able to stop the storm that was to be my life for the next few months.

"Does your father know?" she asked.

"He knows Master da Vinci painted me but not about the exhibit."

"You must start there then, Lisa. Tell him. You owe him at least that much."

I gathered my things and left the monastery. I was too upset for prayer and devotion, for I had to face my mistake and tell Father.

Father had not spoken to me since I had told him what I had done with Master da Vinci.

I waited for Father to return from the bank that day. After I heard him settled into his old chair, I came down the stairs and stood in front of him.

"Father?"

"Yes," he said irritably, plainly still not pleased with me.

I told him about the exhibit for Lady Alfonsina Medici's birthday and of my painting being displayed before all of Florence.

As I said the words I saw pain flash across Father's face. He rose from his seat and opened his mouth to say something, then sat down heavily. A shadow crept over his face, his hand clutched his chest, and he slumped over in his chair.

"Father!" I screamed. I reached out to feel his skin. It was sallow and clammy to the touch.

"No. No, Father!"

The servants came in and Nelda took charge, ordering Father be brought to his room and our carriage sent to fetch the doctor. I sent a messenger to Bea and Franco telling them about Father and they were soon at my door. Bea arrived first, her face lined with concern for me. Forgetting our enmity, she reached out and held my hand for a time, and we were again as sisters.

"I'm afraid, Bea," I whispered.

"You needn't be," she whispered back. "We shall pray," she said calmly.

"I thought you didn't believe God hears prayer," I said.

A trace of a smile showed on her face. "Have we not learned to bring all things to God?" she said as if she was reciting a lesson we learned from the nuns at Santa Trinia.

I smiled, knowing she was well meaning.

"I will stay as long as you need me," she said and excused herself to bring me some warm broth from the kitchen.

Franco arrived next and spoke to the doctor and servants and then came to my rooms and sat across from me in a chair beside the fire. He was quietly looking at me, his eyes warm and misting with emotion.

"Come, sit with me," he said gently.

I rose from my chair and sat leaning against him and I could feel a sense of relief settle over me.

"The doctor has said your father will be fine. And he shall have a full recovery," he assured me. "Are you alright?" he asked.

"I am alright," I said but knew it was only because he was beside me. We sat quietly watching the fire in companionable silence for a while, but he soon announced he had to depart for an early start in the morning.

"Send for me if there is a change in your father's condition," he said.

"I will send for you if there is need," I said. I tried to sound confident, but my voice was thin and apprehensive.

"I will be waiting for you," he said, suddenly tender for he realized I was afraid. "I will always come if you have need of me," he vowed. He said his farewell and departed.

Bea came back to my rooms with a bowl of broth, bread, and cheese, and seeing she could not lift my mood, she bade me rest and then promised to return tomorrow and soon departed.

And I was alone again. Despite Bea and Franco's encouragement, I went into Father's rooms for the rest of the evening, refusing to leave Father's bedside. Finally, the doctor gave me something to help me sleep and I was taken to my room.

The next morning I woke and went downstairs and Father Ficino was in our kitchen eating breakfast. Fear rose up in me and my heart began pounding in my chest at the sight of him. I reasoned he could only be here for one thing. "Why are you here, Reverend?" I said.

He saw the panic on my face and rose from his chair. "Don't worry," he said, taking my hand. "I was summoned by your lord father, and he is doing well, my child. The doctor says it was just a scare."

"Can I speak to him?"

"Let him rest for a while. Come, come and sit with me, for I believe my true purpose here is to speak with you." I followed him out to my garden and sat beside him on one of the benches.

"I have spoken to your father," he said, looking out over the garden. "Well, what he was able to tell me."

"So then you know what I have done," I said.

"I know what he has told me, but do you understand?" He turned to look at me as his grey hair fell across his face. "There is no sin in what you have done, but there is a cost. A cost to you and to those who care for you. So you must decide if it is truly worth it." He spoke evenly with little emotion and then brushed the hair from his face and waited for my response.

"Up until now I've done things," I began slowly, "selfish things, things I'm not proud of. I never really thought about who I was hurting. It all seemed to make sense when I thought I was getting what I wanted. But when father fell ill . . ." My voice faltered.

Father Ficino took my hand to comfort me, and I drew near him and rested my head against his great bulk.

"I thought he might not make it, that I would lose him, and I'm not willing to pay that cost, Reverend." It hit me all at once. The tears began to stream down my face and I sobbed uncontrollably for a long time.

I didn't know how long I sat there crying on Father Ficino's shoulder, but maybe it was the thought of losing Father that made me understand for the first time how my decisions really affected everyone. Maybe this was what I needed to grow up and take responsibility for myself.

I stood up and thanked Father Ficino and then walked upstairs to see Father. I entered his room and knelt down and looked up into his sleeping face. He was so still, for a moment I feared he wasn't breathing, but then he stirred and opened his eyes and looked down into mine. I read concern on his face for me and not the anger I so deserved.

I forced a smile and I spoke. "I did this, Father, and it is my fault and my fault alone. You warned me, but I wouldn't hear you. You told me, but I willfully disobeyed. So I alone should bear the disgrace, Father." His eyes filled with tears and somehow he looked much older and frailer than I remember.

"We will face this together," he assured softly. "I intend on demanding Master da Vinci release the painting to me. He should be driven from Florence, for he has stirred up much rumor and gossip since his return from Milan, in a manner unbefitting our city." He closed his eyes to rest once again.

"No, Father, it is time I grew up, time I took responsibility for my actions." I rose and straightened my dress and ran my fingers through my hair so I would be presentable. "I know what I must do," I said, not really speaking to Father but so I could hear myself say it, so my resolve would not falter.

I found myself walking toward Master da Vinci's house. I didn't remember why I thought another try at begging would work, but I no longer cared how that would make me look. I just knew I had resolved to not leave his house until he agreed with me.

Chapter 13

When I arrived at his house the door was open and I walked in to find no one there, so I went through the hallway that opened to the large room that served as Master da Vinci's workspace. A shock ran through me as I saw the servants loading his paintings on a covered wagon. Was I too late? Had he already begun to load the paintings he would exhibit?

"I am too late," I said bitterly.

Suddenly Maria walked in through the wide doors of his workspace as though she had heard me. She held my gaze for a second and then she said, "What is it, girl? What do you want?"

I felt my cheeks redden but I reined in my anger. "I would speak with Master da Vinci," I said.

"He is not here," she said sourly.

"When will he return?" I asked.

She picked up one of the baskets the servants were loading and turned away from me. I ran after her. My long strides ate up the space between us and I grabbed ahold of her arm. She pulled away from me so the basket she held was between us.

"Please, signora, please tell me where he is. I must speak with him." My eyes began to fill with tears.

She frowned at my persistence but softened when she saw my tears flowing down my face.

"He has gone, child. He was summoned to Milan by King Louis XII of France himself. So you see, he will not return for some time and certainly not for you."

My mouth hung open in astonishment. She turned away again but I did not attempt to stop her.

It took me only a moment to puzzle out what had happened.

Franco's father had saved me.

I would learn later that Franco's father had persuaded Charles d'Amboise, the French governor of Milan, to hire Master da Vinci for a commission ordered by King Louis of France to design a monument in Milan. Franco's father recommended engaging the famous artist before Pope Julius offered his own commission in Rome. Since Pope Julius and King Louis were bitter enemies, the king agreed to move quickly and, in doing so, saved my reputation and Father's honor.

Chapter 14

As I walked back to my house, I wondered why Franco had treated me with charity. I, who had behaved so poorly on our first meeting. I, who had only allowed him into my life because of his promise to help me.

When I arrived back home Franco was there in the kitchen eating like he had been the first day I had met him. He saw me enter the room and stood to greet me with a wide grin spread across his face. I ran to him and embraced him.

He had saved me, truly saved me, and saying thank you didn't seem like the proper response, so I hugged him with all my strength and kissed him. "I don't know how to repay you," I whispered into his ear.

When Father awoke, Franco and I went to his room and I recounted all that had happened, of how I went to Master da Vinci House only to find that he had been summoned to Milan by King Louis of France and all because Franco's family had intervened on our behalf.

Franco and Father met each other's gaze and the faintest touch of amusement played across Father's face. He turned to me. "What will you do now, dear?" Father said.

In response I leaned over and took hold of Franco's hand.

Father beamed a wide smile and said, "So there is hope for happiness."

Franco and I were married in the spring of the following year. I became the wife of Francesco Giocondo. I have learned kindness and tenderness from his treatment of me and he gave me the freedom I craved to explore the aesthetic beauty of artistry and craftsmanship and made no objection when I wanted to spend my allowance on expensive literature to add to my collection of books.

He was gentle and considerate in his care for me, and I often thought of the good fortune that had brought Francesco to me. He had not been the most handsome of suitors. He had a corpulent shape that suggested he would run to fat as he got older. But I adored him and was unhappy when we were apart, preferring his company for even the simplest of things.

I often reflected on something Master da Vinci had said—that beauty had many expressions, and a painting merely captured one of them. But in my case, it wasn't beauty that had been captured but the journey of my discovery—of what was truly important.

Many years later Francesco and I traveled to France, and I saw the painting again. But now the painting held a different meaning for me. You see, the girl in the painting had believed she knew what beauty was. But that girl had been wrong. Beauty was found in so many other things that a painting could not capture, a beauty whose only mirror was in the eye of the beholder. So I liked to think that the smile on my face in the painting was of me discovering the secrets of my life.

Author's Notes

I've taken several liberties with some of the historical facts in the story of Lisa Giacondo. Lisa was a member of the Gherardini family, a prominent Italian house of nobility from Tuscany, originally part of the early political life of Florence before the rise of the republic (signoria) later ruled by the Medicis.

Francesco Giocondo was much older than Lisa, fifteen years older, in fact. And while he was a successful silk merchant, there would be no strategic reason why Lisa's family would marry their daughter to him, unless it was for love.

Leonardo da Vinci traveled back and forth between the duchies of Milan and Florence, taking the portrait with him and working on it incrementally over the years, never actually finishing it. Since France ruled Milan after the overthrow of Duke Ludovico Sforza, the portrait found its way to the royal collection of art in France. Da Vinci

created many fabulous works, eventually being commissioned to paint the Last Supper in Milan and also being
called to Rome by Pope Giovanni de' Medici, who assumed
the papacy as Pope Leo X.

About the Author

An author and inspirational writer, C. T. Hayes is recognized for crafting compelling stories that delve into personal growth, spiritual awakening, and transformation. Drawing from deep personal experiences and profound insights, C. T. Hayes's writing invites readers into meaningful and memorable journeys within each story.